Fire
Diary

Lily Rosenblatt
illustrations by Judith Friedman

Albert Whitman & Company
Morton Grove, Illinois

To Daddy, in loving memory, who would have been proud.
And to my Joe, who is.
   L.R.

To my father, Alex Friedman.
   J.F.

With special thanks to Drs. David Fox and Shirley Lebovics, Cathy, Midge, Evelyn, and Christy for their criticism and support. To Ava Gawronski, a fire survivor, for believing my story. To Mom, a Holocaust survivor, for believing in her children. And to you, Aliza, Eliana, and Joshie, for believing in your mother.

And with gratitude to Peter Wilms, a deputy chief of the Skokie, Illinois, Fire Department, for sharing his expertise. L.R.

Library of Congress Cataloging-in-Publication Data
Rosenblatt, Lily.
Fire Diary / by Lily Rosenblatt;
illustrated by Judith Friedman.
p. cm.
Summary: With the help of her school counselor, nine-year-old April learns to deal with her fears after her house burns down.
 ISBN 0-8075-2439-5
[1. Fires—Fiction. 2. Fear—Fiction.
3. Diaries—Fiction.]
I. Friedman, Judith, ill. II. Title.
PZ7.R719165Fi 1994   93-45917
[E]—dc20   CIP
                                                  AC

Text © 1994 by Lily Rosenblatt.
Illustrations © 1994 by Judith Friedman.
Design by Sandy Newell.
Text is set in Tekton.

Published in 1994 by Albert Whitman & Company,
6340 Oakton Street, Morton Grove, Illinois 60053.
Published simultaneously in Canada by
General Publishing, Limited, Toronto.
Printed in the United States of America.
10 9 8 7 6 5 4 3 2 1

Late Wednesday

Dear Diary:

We lost everything in the fire. All that Mama, Gramma, and I had left were the nightgowns we were wearing and Gramma's old shawl. I even lost Jake, my favorite tattered, stuffed bunny that I had slept with since I was three.

Dr. Brandon said, "Don't keep it all bottled up inside, April. Put together the bits and pieces and write! Tell it one day at a time."

Well, my stuffed Jake always was the best listener. So I'm going to call this diary after him. From now on, it's Dear Jake.

I woke up with a terrible thirst that night. I got up to get a drink, but I couldn't make it out the door. There was smoke everywhere.

I remember the sounds: walls hissing and crackling, dogs howling, sirens. I sat in the corner of my room for a million hours, a million miles away from Mama and Gramma. My face felt hot. My throat felt like fire.

CRASH! My window! Someone was climbing in! It was hard to see. Then a firefighter came out of the smoke. He was big and yellow and scary-looking with that dark mask. Not at all like the friendly firefighters I'd always waved to.

He held me tightly and carried me down a tall ladder from my window.

   Mama and Gramma were on the ground below, their arms up and open. No more smoke. Only cold air, Mama's big arms, and Gramma's warm shawl. I never wanted to let go again.

   We watched our house—the place where I had had nine birthdays, the house with the best hiding places on the block. Now it was just a hot, angry monster, drinking up the firefighters' water, spitting out more flames.

   Gramma screamed, "My wedding ring! Let me get my wedding ring!" Mama just held her tighter, not saying a word.

There was our big house crumbling down, and like Gramma, all I could think of were the little things inside. My softball trophy. The heart pin I got from my best friend, Lanie. My silly old sticker collection. More tears spilled from me than water from the firefighters' hose.

The paramedics came, but we didn't need them. Neighbors and strangers offered help, but we didn't move. Finally, Mrs. Naor from across the street pulled us into her house saying, "If you have to watch, do it from inside." In her kitchen I drank enough water to fill a pool. We stayed there all night, all wrapped together, crying, watching from her window. It was the longest night of my life.

When the fire died and the sun came up, we went out again to see if we could find anything undamaged. There was an awful smell. The only thing that hadn't burnt was the plum tree in our backyard. Its fruit was the last bit of color left in that mess of gray and black ashes.

I remember wondering what morning was doing in a place like this.

That's enough remembering for now, Jake.

Dear Jake:

I'm ready to tell you more.

We moved in with Aunt Fani, Uncle Irv, Laura, and Cathy. We share their food. We share their clothes. We share their beds. We have nothing of our own anymore. I don't mind sharing a bed with Laura, though; I wouldn't want to sleep alone.

Mama said, "We're lucky. All we lost were things, not family. We still have each other, and pretty soon we'll have our own home back, too."

It won't be the same home, though, not without the old stuff in it.

But that's Mama. She can look at a chair with no legs and see a sled. Me, I just see a broken chair.

Sunday night

Dear Jake:

At first, Mama and Gramma and I mostly stayed indoors, just trying to settle ourselves. Mama spent a lot of time on the phone. She was always talking about building the new house, about getting money from here or there. She never smiled during those times.

I'd just look out the window for hours. There were kids jumping rope, azaleas still blooming, mail as usual. All as though nothing had happened. But me all different inside.

Bedtime was the worst. The fire always came to get me. I had to stay awake, alert.

I don't feel very good. Just thinking about it hurts.

Friday morning

Dear Jake:

I remember the day Mama announced that we were going back to school and work.

"Please, no!" I begged. "What if something happens to you and Gramma?" I was terrified. Being with Mama and Gramma seemed like the only way to be safe.

But getting Mama to change her mind is like trying to hold back the rain. It always comes down in the end.

School was awful. I felt like a freak. Everyone asked so many nosy questions. "Did the fire touch you?"

"Was it scary?"

And—of all people!—Lanie just stayed away. I wanted to yell, "Fires aren't contagious!"

During math class, I heard a siren outside. I felt dizzy and queasy. It was hard to breathe.

The teacher took me down to an office marked DR. PAULA BRANDON. Dr. Brandon came out and said, "Hi, April. I'm the school psychologist."

A talking doctor, I thought. I didn't want to talk about anything to anyone. "It's okay. I'm fine now," I lied. But my teacher left me there.

Dr. Brandon smiled and opened her door wider. "Come on in," she said. In the corner of her office was the biggest dollhouse I had ever seen, full of little dolls. A kid-sized table stood in the middle of the room, with paper and crayons on top and chairs all around. There was a bookshelf filled with games, puzzles, and books; and the walls were covered with colored pictures by kids.

"Look over here, April." She led me across the room.

"I want you to meet Ms. Tibbitz. She loves kids."

I couldn't believe it, Jake—her real, live rabbit looked just like you! Dr. Brandon even let me hold her. That was the best thing that happened all day.

late Wednesday

Dear Jake:

I went back to Dr. Brandon's, at first only to visit Ms. Tibbitz. Then sometimes I'd color, or play with the dolls, or listen to Dr. B.'s stories. But I never talked. On my fifth visit, she gave me this diary.

I never let Dr. B. see me laugh when she told her jokes. But she noticed. "Don't hold back your April smile," she said. "Laughing can be time-out from your troubles, and that's good. It recharges your batteries."

I still looked away. "Hey," she said, "let's collect funny things and make a funny board."

I've spent the night cutting pictures from magazines and pasting them together in ridiculous combinations. My favorite one is the skinny girl standing on a tree and sniffing the moon with an elephant's nose. It makes me laugh, and I really have time-out from my scary thoughts. At least until bedtime. Goodnight.

late, late Tuesday

Dear Jake:

It's one in the morning, and I can't sleep again. The fire keeps chasing me.

Wait. . . someone's coming.

That was Mama. She asked why I was still awake. I told her the truth. "I'm staying on the lookout."

She said, "April, remember when you fell out of the plum tree? You just picked yourself up and climbed it all over again. Well, this time we all fell. Real hard. But we've got to get up, dust ourselves off, and keep on. If you tire yourself out trying to keep away the bad things, you'll be asleep when the good things come." She winked. "Now let's go try and get some sleep. Tomorrow always brings something new."

Sometimes I wish Mama wouldn't pretend everything was so fine. Sometimes it just isn't.

Wednesday afternoon

Dear Jake:

I finally talked to Dr. B. about last night and all the other nights I stay awake. She told me Mama was right and that "you can't erase the old, scary pictures in your mind, but you can exchange them for happy pictures. Fish out those old happy memories, make happy funny boards, tell a joke.

"And when all else fails," she handed me the crayons, "make a happy picture." Here's what I drew.

"Gotcha!" I yelled when I was done.

Dr. B. clapped and laughed. "Remember that feeling and this picture whenever the fire chases you."

It's hard, Jake, but I'm gonna try . . .

Monday evening

Dear Jake:

Dr. B. and I took a long walk today. Dr. B. notices everything. "That man sure is in a hurry. He forgot to comb his hair"—"Smell that grass. I bet it was just mowed."

We ended up on my old street. Between the frames of the new house being built, we saw my plum tree standing tall. I got that sick, shaky feeling again. Dr. B. held my hand tight. "Look at those two birds arguing over a worm. Isn't that what we silly people look like sometimes?" I tried real hard to concentrate.

"Remember, just change the picture. Just change the picture," Dr. B. said.

Finally, I took a deep breath.

"April, the fire knocked your house down, but you're still here." She hugged me. "You're strong, and you survived—just like that tree."

I turned away. "I just want everything to be like before."

"One step at a time," she said, still eyeing the tree. "We all need branches to climb to the top."

When I got back to Aunt Fani's, I thought about the tree. Lanie and I used to play "time the climb" to see who could climb the fastest to the top. I sat by the phone for a long time. Finally, I dialed. "Lanie, want to come over and see the funny board I made?"

The doorbell rang even before I finished dinner. Lanie and I laughed at my funny board. She even favored the same funny pictures. I let her read parts of my diary. "I'm so sorry, April," she said. "I was just scared. I didn't know what to say to you." I told her, "Lanie, you make it better just by staying my best friend."

Thursday night

Dear Jake:

Our class went to the fire station today. Lanie stuck by me the whole time. Without masks, the firefighters looked friendly again. They showed us their equipment and explained what everything was for. Lanie squeezed my hand tighter when they pulled out the black masks.

"These protect us from the smoke," the firefighter said. "Without them, we couldn't go into a burning house." I never thought those ugly masks would make me smile.

I'm keeping the guidelines handout they gave us in the back of this diary.

It's late now, and it's starting to snow. I'm trying the counting and deep breathing Dr. B. showed me. And remembering the happy pictures.

Innnnn. Ouuuut. Innnnn. Ouuuut.

One . . . Mama and Lanie and me roasting hot dogs on our camping trip.

Two . . . Gramma and me picking a bouquet from our garden to surprise Mama.

Three . . . the first time I swam in the ocean.

I'm really tired now. Goodnight.

Sunday morning

Dear Jake:

It sure feels good to be sleeping through the night. I showed Mama my cowgirl drawing and told her about how I was learning to "change the pictures" in my mind. Suddenly, she started crying and said, "I have trouble with the pictures in my mind, too. I can't even concentrate on my work."

I couldn't believe it. It seemed Mama's sled was turning back into a broken chair. I told her I'd help her make new pictures to remember when the scary ones came.

She looked surprised. Maybe her little girl was learning to fix broken chairs now.

Mama and I drew lots of happy pictures. Then we made an escape poster. Mama drew a diagram of the inside of the new house, and together we planned escape routes for each room. I colored the poster in with bright markers. On the top, I wrote DON'T BE SCARED, BE PREPARED. I knew just where this would go in the new house.

Dear Jake:

It has been a while since I've written, but I've been so busy with school and softball.

You'll never believe where I'm writing this from.

But before that, let me tell you that we moved in today. At first, we stood outside for a long time. Gramma fiddled with a crumpled handkerchief, and Mama cried without one.

"It's okay, April," Mama finally said. "You, me, and Gramma, we made it. We're together. We dusted off and we're back." Gramma reached out, and we all hugged.

Neighbors came by to bring us stuff. Some were old friends, some I'd never met. Mr. Sental came over with some blankets and pillows. Mrs. Naor made us some fried chicken and delicious bread pudding. I guess even a fire can bring about some good.

First thing we did was to check the smoke detectors and make sure they worked. This time they are all over the house; some use batteries and some use electricity. The one in my room is right by my door. Now it can be on the lookout instead of me. I put the escape poster up on the refrigerator for everyone to see. I hung up my funny board in my room right next to the picture of me, the cowgirl, catching the fire monster. Those are good pictures for when I'm having a not-so-good day. I put the flowers Dr. B. sent in a vase by my bed. The house looks better already.

When things quieted down, I came out to the backyard. I sat by the plum tree for a long time. Then I climbed it. And that's where I am right now—at the top.

Show these guidelines to your parent or guardian. They have been prepared with the help of a professional firefighter.

WHAT TO DO BEFORE A FIRE

1. BE PREPARED. Organize a family meeting to discuss and rehearse these guidelines. Schools have fire drills—so should you.

2. Make sure there are working smoke detectors in the kitchen, hall, basement, and adjacent to sleeping areas. There should be at least one detector on each floor of the house.

3. Check doors and windows for easy accessibility. You might consider attaching escape ladders to second-story (or higher) windows.

4. Develop and practice an emergency escape plan. Draw a map of the house with at least two escape routes for each room.

5. Designate a place outside the home where everyone can meet and be accounted for in case of a fire.

WHAT TO DO DURING A FIRE

1. DON'T PANIC. Leave the house IMMEDIATELY. Go to a neighbor's house and dial 9-1-1 for the fire department.

2. Crawl close to the floor. Smoke and heat from the fire rise to the ceiling.

3. Feel a door and/or doorknob before opening it. If it's warm, DO NOT OPEN IT.

4. If your clothing catches fire,
   STOP where you are,
   DROP to the ground,
   ROLL on the ground
   to smother the flames.

5. Do not return to the house for ANY reason.

WHAT TO DO AFTER A FIRE

1. Arrange a family meeting to discuss each person's feelings/reactions/thoughts about the event.

2. It's normal to feel "strange" or "different" after a trauma. Encourage each person in the family to express his or her feelings.

3. It is advisable to seek counseling for both the adults and children, even if only one session, just to have some guidance and professional perspective.